KITTY RIDDLES

by Katy Hall and Lisa Eisenberg

pictures by R.W. Alley

Dial easy-to-read

Dial Books for Young Readers • New York

Published by Dial Books for Young Readers
A division of Penguin Putnam Inc.
345 Hudson Street
New York, New York 10014

Text copyright © 2000 by Kate McMullan and Lisa Eisenberg
Pictures copyright © 2000 by R. W. Alley
Printed in USA

The Dial Easy-to-Read logo is a registered trademark of
Dial Books for Young Readers,
a division of Penguin Putnam Inc.
® TM 1,162,718.
First Edition
3 5 7 9 10 8 6 4 2

Library of Congress Cataloging in Publication Data
Hall, Katy.
Kitty riddles/by Katy Hall and Lisa Eisenberg;
pictures by R. W. Alley.—1st ed.
p. cm.
Summary: A collection of riddles about cats, including
"Which famous kitty ruled Egypt? Cleocatra!" and
"How do kitties cut their grass? With a lawn meower!"
ISBN 0-8037-2116-1
1. Riddles, Juvenile. 2. Cats—Juvenile humor.
[1. Cats—Wit and humor. 2. Riddles. 3. Jokes.]
I. Eisenberg, Lisa. II. Alley, R. W. (Robert W.), ill. III. Title.
PN6371.5.H3485 2000
818'.5402—dc21 97-37438 CIP AC

Reading Level 2.6

The full-color artwork was prepared
using ink and watercolor.

Dedicated to Groucho,
the best kitty in the
world
—K.H.
In memory of Puck
—L.E.

To Tanya and Fluffy
—R.W.A.

What do you call a kitty with a can of tuna?

Purr-fectly happy!

Why did the baby cat carry
around a box of Band-Aids?

She wanted to be a first-aid kit!

What do kitties like to put on their mouse-burgers?

Cats-up!

What did the kitty say when
the mouse got away?

Oh, rats!

What kind of kitties are the
best bowlers?

Alley cats!

Which famous kitty ruled
Egypt?

Cleocatra!

How do kitties cut their grass?

With a lawn meower!

What kind of kitty has eight
legs?

An octo-puss!

14

Why do kitties sing so well?

They're very mewsical.

Where do kitties find out
what's happening?

From the *Daily Mews*!

What mountains do kitties
love?

The Catskills!

Do kitties like to shop in
stores?

No, they prefer catalogs!

What do kitties eat for breakfast?

Mice Krispies and Puffed Mice!

19

What ancient land had the happiest cats?

Purr-sia!

What do you call a kitty that eats a duck?

A duck-filled fatty puss!

What do you call a fight
between two kitties?

A cat-astrophe!

Why did the kitty let the genie out of the bottle?

She was hoping she'd be granted three fishes!

23

What's little and soft and says,
"Beow! Beow!"

A kitty with a cold!

Can your pet kitty ever learn to like your pet bird?

Yes, especially with barbecue sauce!

What's a kitty's favorite color?

Purrple!

How should you pet an angry, wet kitty?

From fur, fur away!

How do cats find out they're going to be parents?

They get a litter!

Who's the most famous cat
from the Wild West?

Kitty Carson!

What do kitties do on the
Fourth of July?

They march in big purr-ades.

What game do kitties play at birthday parties?

Mewsical chairs!

Why did the kitty move to a
new neighborhood?

Because the old one was
going to the dogs!

What do you get if you cross a kitty and a snapping turtle?

Cat nip!

What kind of kitty wears
sunglasses and a raincoat and
says, "Bow wow"?

An impawstor.

What do you call a kitty with pigtails?

A braidy-cat!

Is it really unlucky to see a
black cat?

Only if you're a mouse!

What prize did the movie star kitty hope to win?

The A-cat-emy Award!

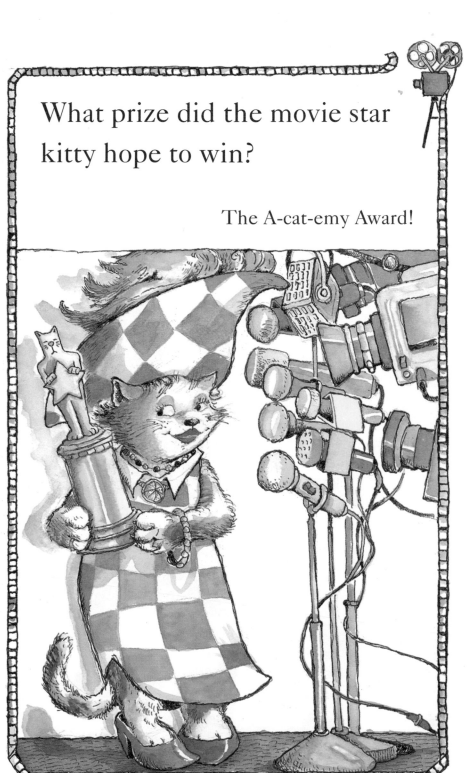

What are kitty's favorite
subjects in school?

Mewsic, Hisstory, Fureign
Languages, and Fishing.

What do you get if you cross a
cat with a laughing hyena?

A giggle puss.

When it rains cats and dogs,
what do kitties avoid?

Poodles.